Jill Dow trained at the Royal College of
Art. Since graduating she has worked as a
freelance illustrator specializing in natural
history, including the highly successful
series *Bellamy's Changing World*.
The *Windy Edge Farm* stories are the
first books she has both written
and illustrated.

Jill Dow lives in Thornhill, near Stirling,
Scotland, with her husband and their
two young children.

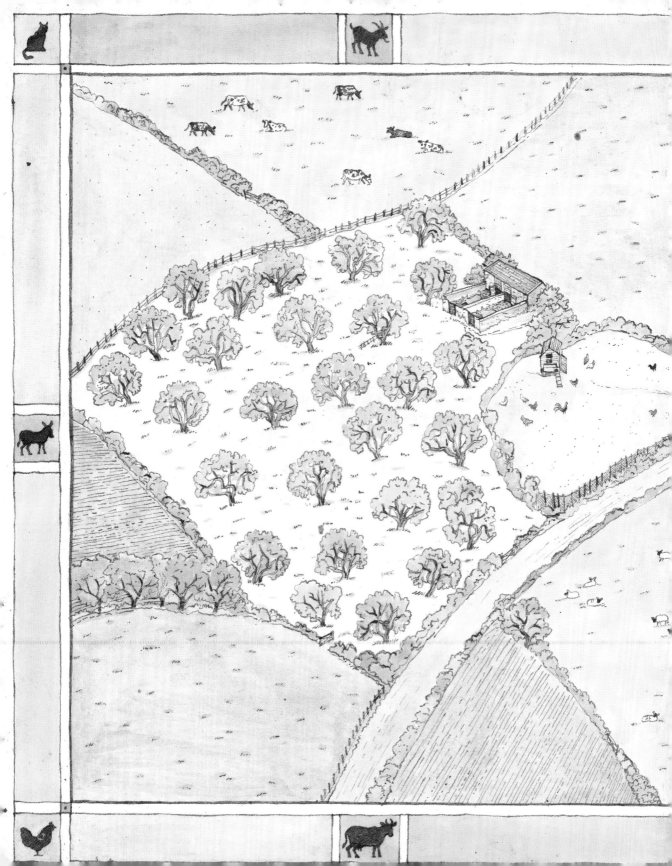

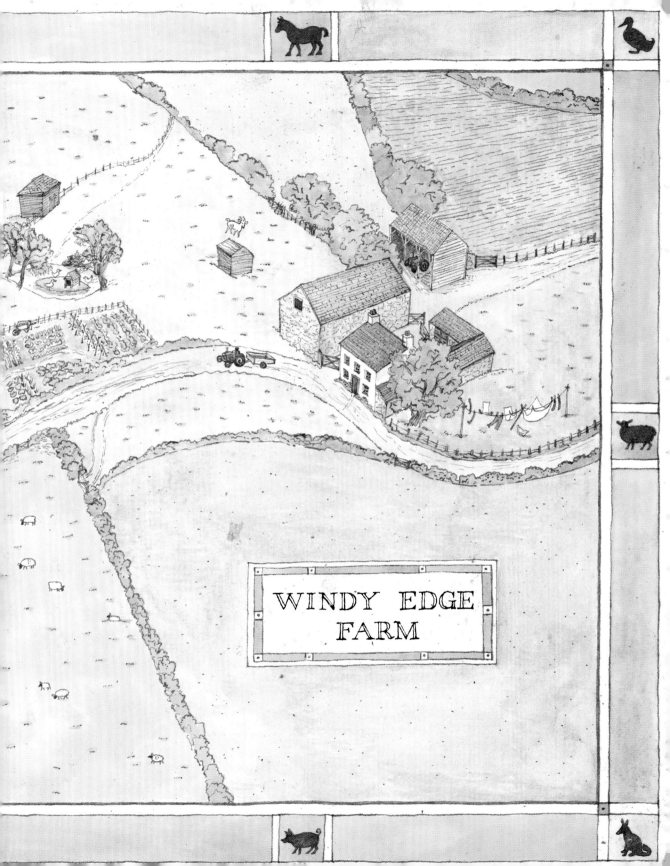

WINDY EDGE
FARM

For Kirsty and Ben

Molly's Supper
© Frances Lincoln Limited 1989
Text and illustrations © Jill Dow 1989

First published in 1989 by
Frances Lincoln Limited, Apollo Works,
5 Charlton Kings Road, London NW5 2SB

ISBN 0-7112-0587-6 hardback
ISBN 0-7112-0569-8 paperback

5 7 9 8 6

Printed and bound in Hong Kong

Design and art direction   Debbie MacKinnon

WINDY EDGE FARM

MOLLY'S SUPPER

Jill Dow

FRANCES LINCOLN

The walls of Windy Edge Farmhouse glowed pink in the light of the setting sun. High in the barn, the owl woke. She ruffled her feathers and stretched out her wings before flying off to spend the night hunting.

Molly, the little white cat with ginger and black patches, had been out hunting all day at the other end of the farm.

Here, in the furthest field, young rabbits played on the banks, and whole families of voles scuttled under the hedges.

But Molly had been unlucky. She had not caught anything to eat all day, and now she was feeling very hungry.

Molly wished she hadn't strayed so far away from the farmyard, where right now the farmer would be feeding all the other animals. She set off for home as fast as she could.

She jumped over the gate into the meadow, and scampered past the donkeys.

"Good evening," they said, between mouthfuls of thistle and buttercup, but Molly didn't stop to reply. If she didn't hurry, she would miss her supper.

In the shadowy orchard, the sheep were already settling down under the trees for the night. *They* weren't hungry, because they had been eating grass all day long. They were still chewing silently as Molly rushed by.

As she ran along the pigsty wall, Molly saw that the pigs had already been fed. Their snouts were buried deep in their troughs, and their happy grunts only made the little cat feel even more hungry.

It was suppertime for the hens too. They ran clucking from all directions to peck at the grain Angus scattered for them. Molly stopped to see if there was any food for *her*. But grain was not a very good meal for a cat, so off she ran –

round the duckpond,
where the ducks were
climbing out of the water
and tucking their heads
under their wings,

and past the goatshed, where Clover and Hazel were munching hay and green leaves.

"What's the rush?" they asked each other, as Molly and her shadow dashed past their door.

When Molly reached the barn, she squeezed in through a hole in the wall. Mr Finlay had just finished milking the cows, and now he was filling their stalls with hay. The fresh, warm milk smelled delicious, and Molly couldn't resist dipping her paw in to have a taste. But the farmer shouted loudly at her, and waved his pitchfork in the air. Poor Molly ran away frightened, without tasting a single drop.

Molly was nearly home, but she still had to pass the dogs' kennel. With flattened ears she crept by, keeping low. She hoped the dogs wouldn't notice her, but they did!

They looked up from gnawing their bones and barked gruffly. "You'd better hurry, cat, or you'll be too late."

At last Molly arrived at the back doorstep. But the other cats were already licking their plates clean, and washing their faces contentedly.

Poor tired, hungry Molly! She *was* too late for supper, after all. She miaowed loudly with disappointment, and scratched with her front paws on the kitchen door to show Mrs Finlay just how upset she was.

"Late again, Molly!" said Mrs Finlay, opening the door. "Where have you been this time?"

Molly could smell something delicious. She dashed inside, and there on the kitchen floor was a plate of fish and a saucer of milk.

"Aren't you glad I always save your supper for you, Molly?" asked Mrs Finlay.

But the little patchy cat didn't answer. She was far too busy, eating and purring at the same time.

– The End –